MY UNFORGETTABLE LOVE NIGHTS WITH THE WITCH

ARIAN S. TOWNSEND

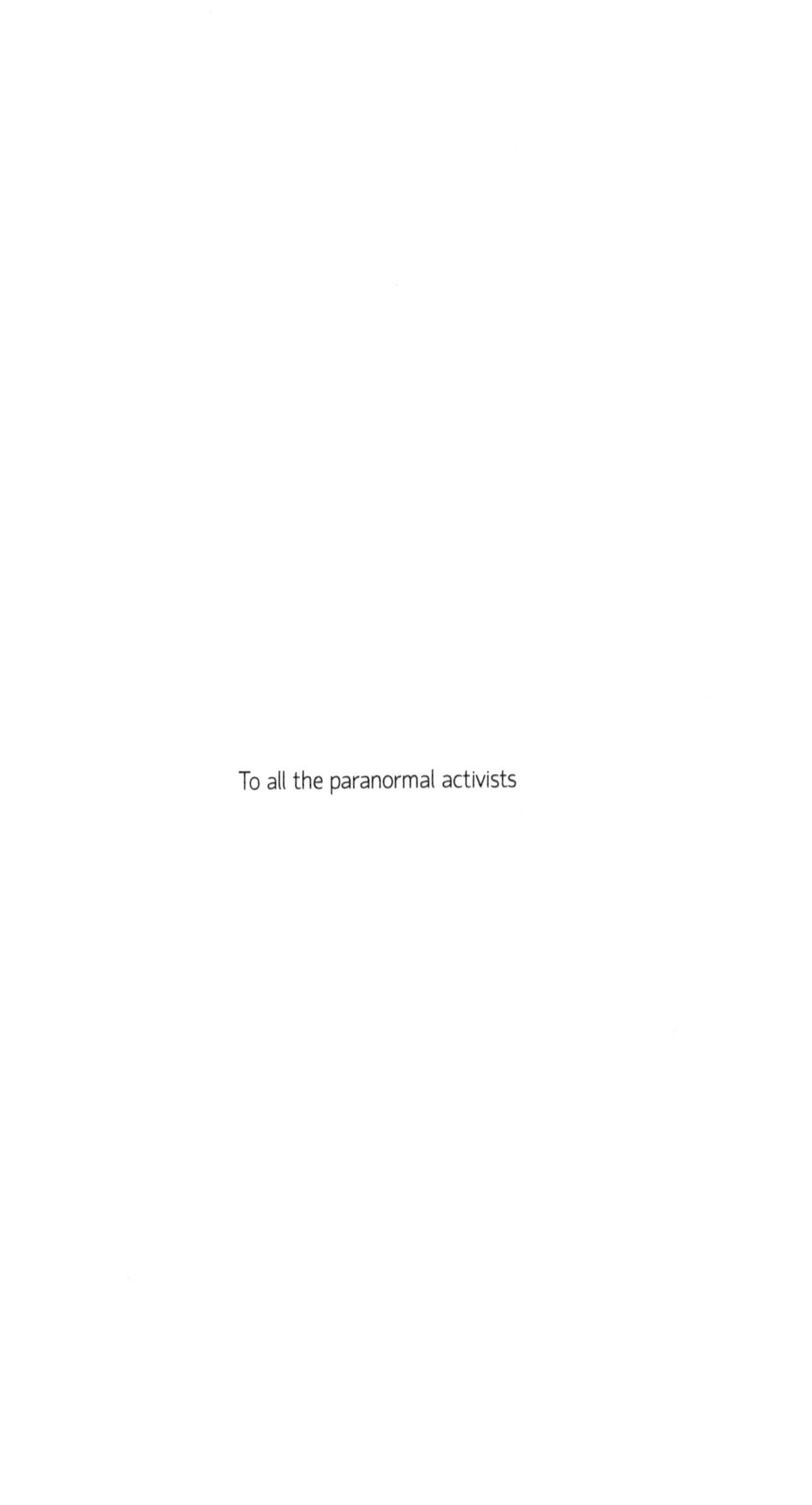

To all the paranormal activists

Contents

Foreword

There are more things in this world whic is beyong explanation. The present fiction is one such, based on personal experience.

Preface

Mystery lies evanywhere, only you need the eye to look at it.

Acknowledgements

To all myreaders

Prologue

The earth is full of beauty and mystery. If you know, you will believe, if you don't know, you will not believe it.

- Aren't you afraid? I laughed a little when I heard Alina's words. I said - What do you think of my fear? Why should I fear at all? She says nothing to me but stared at. The other side of the window is Pretty dark. I look deeply at her I do not understand why I think I know and she has deep eyes. Looking at Her eyes, there is one Wonder is working. Who says only humans are surprised Maybe !! The incorporeal ones are also amazed Maybe it's not the look of living ones I could see and understand! Alina pierced through the window in to my room. As we remove the curtain of the door and enter the house just like that. The matter seems to be very normal like any incident. If anyone else would have been here he would have screamed at fear but I managed. But this did not happen by chance! I have been renting here for a long time No. When I first came here for rent I was a little surprised to hear the rent. On top of that when despite of my being Bachelor, the landlord agree to rent me the apartment really make me a little surprised!

Usually the owners do not want to rent the bachelors. There are other families in other floors of the house. All the other floors are Rented only this one is left. Though I had a little doubt then but I thought myself that From all The big advantage is the house from my office Very close to. It is only walking distance, so I could save the bus fare. Some days were going well. Only The problem was that my house was at night It would have been a little cold. It it was less, it Would have been better It was scorching hot outside but I did Relax in the cold without turning on the AC I got it. Another thing is the owner of the house Come every morning to find my news and well being, he would ask whether I have a problem and Whether or not I'm fine! In the face of the landlord when speaking To me I usually see the impression of a different kind of anxiety that I got to see. But when I said to him, no No problem then from the gentleman's appearance It looked like that from the top of his chest a stone as if moved away. I have had some doubts since.

Now only when suspicion is created I could easily go to the owner of the house and ask clearly that's what Uncle, are there ghosts in your house! And if you want to know, why he should tell you? The house owner Can tell me to leave. Why II should leave such a wonderful place !! But one day near the shop in the neighborhood I wanted to know. First of all, the shopkeeper boy Needless to say was not ready to divulge anything.

But I'm in that flat for over two weeks and The shopkeeper found me quite comfortable there so He looked at me in surprise. Then he lowered his voice and said what he said, The bottom line is that I live in a flat There is a ghost in that flat. Not exactly ghosts or female ghosts. In plain language witch ! The girl died there many years ago. The girl's name was Alina! Before that, there was only one person in that flat but he couldn't stay more than a week. This is how I've been for a couple of weeks There is no end to his wonder. I laughed and blew away. I bought my grocery and came home! As soon as I got home I did the things I started to think a little! No matter how much you laugh I blow a little in my mind Fear or doubt is created by then Gone! There really is something here at this home! Especially cold issues.

Moreover, another thing I didn't notice before but need to notice It seems to have been. I still eat outside mostly as I do before also. But sometimes at the moment of extreme hunger, the moment when I did not wish not to go out Then something is made at home. These happened almost twice a week. When I was hungry at night Once Bombay toast and mixed rice I cooked. I left the dish in the basin thinking that I shall wash it in the morning. In the morning As a result of leaving to office early, it was not done anymore. But when I come home I see them perfectly cleaned, I remember later Maybe I was the one who cleaned them Done! I do not remember! Let me think no more. Whatever it really is Then she will do me no harm No, I understand that clearly! If you were afraid, then so many days It would have been the same!

I see Alina for another week Later. I'm back from the office just then. There was a lot of work that day . About 10 o'clock at night when I came home . As soon as I entered the house, my head seemed to be moving, No. I start to open clothes from the door. The goal is just to bed! After all I First need to sleep for an hour then may be I can think about other things! I came after eating. So no worries. I took off my shoes and socks Towards the bedroom As soon as I was walking, it was cold from behind One of the voices said - Why are you so messy? I could say something for a while No. Absolutely silent! I noticed my foot It's a little shaky. Maybe mine At first it was necessary to think that someone else Entered my room. But in the voice There was something about that my whole body Trembled! By then the room temperature a lot has come down. My whole body as if, It was getting cold! I tried to explain myself That it won't hurt me. No harm done! This is a good one Ghost! Good night! Sweet witch !!

Too much fear grasped me and the good thinking was not of much work. Strong desire Was to close the door towards the front room that occurs to me but I suppressed the desire! With a lot of courage I Get ready to look behind! I turned around and saw there none. But the clothes I threw away And the shoes and socks are also arranged orderly. I think the girl is gone. Because the temperature of the room again Has begun to rise. Then I heard the invisible voice of the girl A few times. Every time mild gentle rule for my disorder! I discovered that the girl was mild And not afraid at all! Yesterday before I went to the office I left a small note On my messy shirt! "I want to see you" Somewhat ridiculous to myself Sounds like that as if I'm with a pet Want to meet!

What the People will think when they will heard? Who knows! Even after returning from the office I couldn't find it. But my shirt The food was just tidy! The window before going to bed at night I looked at a shadow I saw the statue. My chest trembled but I managed to push inside Soon! I went ahead on my own In front. The shadow is still clearly visible. There is silence on the other side! Before me I wanted to know - Are you here? That's when Alina wanted to know! When the girl came in the light of the house I noticed with little surprise I have not seen such a beautiful face for a long time! I have no time to talk I couldn't! Just waiting! She said - you really like the look on ghost's face? Se started laughing very loudly! I said - Can't believe it! Our childhood What is taught about ghosts. I see that it is completely opposite to female ghosts! She looked at me and said - You look so brave! Before you, The people came to live here were quite scared! Well done Talk to you soon and keep up the good content. - You can make love with me if you want! -Well! So? -you know the advantage of making love with beautiful female ghost love? What? -What do you hear? -the witches's father cannot to marry her against her wish! Get married Not likely to go! After saying this, I saw her face, The face just got little sad! She Said looking at me - Well, I'll go! - why! Where? My words hurt you? - No, that's right! - No, that's not right. Tell me then Go! I was surprised to hear my own voice what I have said. I'm with a ghost Arguing.

That's the way I say it I don't know if she laughs again Fell! Then she looked at me Said - Whatever you think we are, in fact Not we are not so free! Just like you We have our own world You have your own world. We have to stay there in our world too! -Then in our world !! -Actually those whose deaths are normal A connection of this world with them are made! We are here even if we want to To keep themselves away from we can't! Got it! I do not want! -Hmm. Got it! When will it come again? - Really! Let's go now! Not much is known about her, however The girl will come again! Then with her I can hang out! She went away as she had come that is piercing the window. I went to bed to sleep For! Well, what do you think of us? Did you say? -Will I think again? So many days I heard so I will remember! - What did you hear? Where did you hear that? -

That doesn't mean anything is true! -Of course not! -Then? This is why so many people die How? -Wonder how they die! We don't know! Themselves What do we have to do if they die in fear? .Do we have nothing to do that I will scare you! Huh !! I said -Well, how is your world? Then she said - How can I say! Well listen, Let me tell you something. Our world is but a lot Just like you You can say one There is a parallel world like your world That's right. - I don't understand! Lately I have only thing foe which I come home The job is to talk to her. The girl is just like me Waiting. I'm actually at home I see the bathroom is hot for me The water is waiting. I take a bath I can feel the temperature in my room How cold it has become. I understand she has left without any trouble.

Before So we're just in my bedroom but now I used to talk everywhere in the house now The two of us walked together. Watching TV or when electricity is gone, she sat on the verandah Let's talk. Sometimes I Surprised with an incorporeal being how can I talk so much! How I say !! Another thing that has happened is Alina bring something from her world, it is just like as we eat mango juice just like that pack Is done. What a strange language on its pack is written! To know about it, I wanted to know what she said That's one of their food. She brings it hidden for me. We eat juice by inserting such pipes she also started eating by inserting straw pipe as I did. Honestly, it's weird I have never eaten such a thing before but I eat it during the day and I told her to bring it every day I told her to bring it. And At the same time our chat going on!

Her hand raised to explain to me. Then she began to say - Look at us and you But the world is much the same! When Someone gets rid of his body That's when he went to my world Entering or the way to enter Finds! It can be said that he is inside The power of entry is gone. And The truth is that once this If it enters the earth They do not remember anything else! I said -Then you are in this world again Why? - I don't remember saying one day ago. In fact those are the ones after a little accident died they can not evade the attraction of this world just like they Can't get their salvation is just like that Not so between the two worlds Let's go! Got it! -Hmm! Got it!

My boy, is your body okay? I leaned towards the landlord. Let's look. I wondered who he was Maybe stop looking for me Give that especially when you see that I'm not afraid. On top of that I am taking any name to leave his house No. But my idea is a bit wrong The landlord has to prove it I started searching regularly . One day he asked me directly Did that - Are you in good health? - Uncle, I am fine! -Sleep well at night? - Yes! -Oh! No matter how your body is getting worse day by day, so know I asked! - No. Actually in the office there is little pressure Lately! -Okay! Listening to me, the landlord seemed not to like exactly my words. He also does not believe my words exactly and I don't think he did. At least his eyes It seems so! But one thing is certain that my health is deteriorating day by day, How about my own Looked like. Lately everyone is saying mine Or the body is getting worse. What is the reason, I can't even catch it myself. Why my health is worsening, I can't say! Anyway, mine relationship with Alina As if the relationship is a little further step forward. She is in my home and works All work! She Let me do nothing! Putting everything in the right place Lets! And that weird juice every day Come on! I'm pretty good! Sometimes Sometimes it seems like a good house wife How much better it would have been if I had one like her! I just thought about it she told me the same day! With a lot of sadness, she said that it is possible which seems to be very strange to me. Which is too much for me to hear I was surprised! Not surprisingly I said in surprise -Is it possible? -Hmm! If you want Do you really want to? That's the thing! I just said -I want! Definitely want! I know why I think she is mine I was very happy to hear that. A little So happy! The proposal is such that it is in her favor It is possible to come to her world like before No, but for me or her It is possible to go to earth and do like her However, for a temporary period! I could not understand how I will do the work! She said it is just to understand her and me inside, The difference is my body! Now The work will be my soul To separate from the body! If Only then can I separate it will be Possible! What she told me meant The human soul is attached to the body

There is only the force of the mind binds it! The mind is subconsciously stressed and stuck himself inside the body. Now the emphasis is on my mind I have to create so that I can I have to get my soul out of body and the soul will be separated from! Try hard every day before going to bed, she said and I started doing it! But where is the key! Even after trying for a week like this There was no profit for I see her all in Tears welled up in her eyes I saw! She is in a lot of trouble and Just told me - Her wish to live was not fulfilled and now her only wish after death is not fulfilled either.

I know why her face is mixed with tears I Can't stand it! I am very angry with myself! Something happened that day! Exactly at night I woke up at three o'clock! I wake up and look around Something like a dim light Is playing. But as far as I'm concerned Was in my room at some point It is not completely dark! There is a light in the house next door The light stays on all night. How strange the light seemed! At least I have not seen such light in my whole life! There is no explanation for this light It is not possible to give! But slowly Slowly I realized the place Actually my bedroom. This is weird It looks different because of the light. I looked around and moved a little It's as if I'm too light I think so! My eyes looked down Ascended to the sky! Someone is lying just below There is that person who looks exactly like me. Even I fall asleep at night I was wearing that dress. I look at it with some disbelief I looked at it. So? Then really! Done? Now you can go to Alina's world? To enter the land of her, Can I? What can I really do! That's when I'm going to move a little I saw something like a rope With just from my feet Stuck. And that's my body, Stuck at the feet of the body! A lot It's like a shackle. With that I am really bound, I'm stuck with the body! I stretched for a while but There was no gain. It did not open or I did not see any signs of opening! That's right At that time I saw her. She is with an axe with white blade in hand Something weird looking! Looking at me she Smiles! But why inside her laughter I know I did not see any soul. Rather, there is a kind of Hurry up! She said - It has to be cut! - There will be no harm! -No! No problem! Mine Do not rely on words! I must think a little more I wanted to! Now cut What's up? I think I know why it is bothering me, Being that it is mine with my body The bond of the soul. This is not just the mind The main thing that makes me my body Stuck with If it is now When I broke up? I can go back In my body?

Just at that moment, The door to the bedroom slammed open. I looked at the door and saw there With the landlord standing Another one! I know him very well Not much trouble. Our area priest of the church! Someone opened the door for me Did not look. Such a feeling As if they can't see me! Their eyes are on my sleeping body Towards! The landlord became very excited One said. But I vaguely I heard. It seemed like a long way off I can hear from! Only one word went to the ears! The landlord says Is it late? The priest said - I don't think so! The body is still hot! Then he knelt towards my body He came forward and touched his hand. With that touch my whole body trembled! I looked at Alina and saw her face sad and is depressed. Then the priest sorinkled Water on me. I do not remember anything! I wake up quite early in the morning I got up. I looked and saw the landlord He is looking at me. Mine One in his face to open his eyes A line of sadness was reduced a little! I just don't understand what happened. And what is the landlord doing in my house. How vague the events of the night are Fuzzy I remember. A little later the priest of the nearby church came and Saw me. They said to Me last night's incident!

Pretty late at night I screamed and screamed. That Hearing the landlord at my door Came to the front. He is already I guess something happened to Mine. Go straight to church priest Call! The priest wanted to know - How long do you talk to that girl? - Over a month! - Would she give you something to eat? I mean, bring it with you! -Hmm! - That's what made her boss on you. Anyway, much better now There is. If at the time we would not come, a lot of damage Could happen surely. You may not survive anymore! Don't stay here anymore. I left the apartment that day. Things Let me be the only one for the time being I went out with a bag to a friend, I go home without looking for another home Until I restore myself!

How much money is there left in my bag? As soon as I opened it, I saw inside my clothes A piece of paper inside! There Just write a line "To you I Wanted to get closer, maybe a little, This is my only crime " There is nothing else written! I folded the paper and I threw it out! Rather than Witches' love, Survival is much better for mine and I felt more happy!